Martin and the Teacher's Pets

by Bernice Chardiet and Grace Maccarone
Illustrated by G. Brian Karas

Hello Reader! — Level 3

SCHOLASTIC INC. Cartwheel ·B·O·O·K·S·®
New York   Toronto   London   Auckland   Sydney
Mexico City   New Delhi   Hong Kong

Ms. Darcy's class was getting ready
for a long holiday weekend.
Everyone wanted to take home
Ms. Darcy's classroom pets.
Sammy was taking the rabbit.
Cynthia was taking the hamster.
John was taking the turtles.

"Who will take the goldfish?"
Ms. Darcy asked.
"Yuck," said Brenda. "Fish smell."
"My cat would eat them," said Bunny.
"I only like dogs," said Raymond Allen
Tally, who was also known as RAT.

Martin loved the goldfish.
"I'll take them," he said.
"Good!" said Ms. Darcy. "But you must
get permission from your parents."

That night Martin asked for permission.
"Taking care of fish is a big job,"
his father said. "You'll have to
feed them and clean their tank."

"You'll have to keep them healthy and safe,"
said his mother.
"I will," said Martin. "I promise."
"Then the answer is yes," said Martin's father.

On Friday, Ms. Darcy told Martin
what to do. "Feed the fish once a day.
If they go to the top of the tank for air,
give them fresh water.
Don't let their water get too hot
or too cold or too dirty."
Martin listened very carefully.

At three o'clock,
Martin's mother came
to help him take the fish home.

Martin set up the tank at once.
He watched the fish play.
Bubbles swam through the hole in the rock.
Max pushed a pebble along the bottom
of the tank.
Swimmy swam around in a circle.
Martin ran a finger along the side
of the tank. Speckles followed it.

Martin watched the fish until bedtime.
"Good night, fish," Martin said as he
turned off the light.
In the dark, he could still hear
the sound of a pebble being pushed
along the bottom of the tank.

As soon as he woke,
Martin went to look at the fish.
The fish looked right back.
Speckles seemed to know him.

Speckles was big and beautiful, and
Martin wanted to show him off.
Carefully, Martin took Speckles out of
the tank and put him in a bucket.

"My bucket! Mine!" Martin's sister, Lisa,
yelled as Martin walked out the door.
"I'll bring it back soon," Martin promised.

Martin walked across the street.
Bunny and Brenda were on the swings
in Brenda's yard.
Bunny said hello to Speckles.
Brenda held her nose.

Martin walked around the block.
RAT and his big dog, Animal,
were coming down the street.
RAT laughed. "Why are you carrying
that dumb fish around?"
"Fish are not dumb," Martin said.
"And I can prove it."
"Oh, yeah?" RAT said. "Do they
fetch? Do they play ball? Show me!"

Just then, Animal put his head into
the bucket.
Martin screamed. "Your dog is eating
my fish!"

RAT pulled Animal's nose
out of the bucket.
Speckles was still there.
"Animal didn't want to eat that
dumb fish," RAT said. "He just
wanted a drink of water."

All of a sudden,
Animal ran after a bird.
RAT ran after Animal.
Martin went back home.

Lisa followed Martin into his room.
"My bucket! Mine!" she said.
Just then, the doorbell rang.

Martin put down the bucket
and ran to the door.
It was Sammy.
He was very excited.

"Mike Dooley is signing books
at the bookstore," Sammy said.
"My dad is waiting in the car.
We've got to go right now!"
Mike Dooley was the boys'
favorite football player.

"I'm going to the bookstore with
Sammy and his dad," Martin called
to his mother. "Okay?"
"Okay," said his mom.
Martin raced out the door.

The bookstore was crowded.
Martin and Sammy got in line.
RAT was in line, too.
"Where's your dumb fish?" he asked.

Martin began to worry.
He wished he had put Speckles
back in the fish tank.

Martin was finally at the front of the line.
And Mike Dooley was signing a book for him.
But Martin could only think of Speckles.

When the boys returned to Martin's house,
Speckles was gone.
"Where's Speckles?" Martin asked Lisa.
"Where's my fish?"

Lisa pointed to the bathroom door.

"Fish in there," she said.

Martin ran to the bathroom.

The door was shut.

Martin banged on the door.
"Mom! Wait! Don't!"
But it was too late.

Martin heard a flush, then running water.
When his mother came out, Martin and
Sammy rushed in.
"Oh no! He's gone!" said Martin.
"What am I going to do?"

"You'd better buy Ms. Darcy a new fish,"
Sammy said.
"I know," said Martin. "But it won't be
the same. It won't be Speckles."

On the way to the pet store, the boys
saw Brenda and Bunny and told them
what happened to Speckles.
"We'll help you find a new fish for
Ms. Darcy," Bunny said.
"Yuck," said Brenda.
"We can call him Speckles the Second,"
said Bunny.

"We want a goldfish with orange,
black, and white spots," Martin said
to the pet store man.
"Here are the goldfish," said the man.
"Pick whichever one you want."

In the tank were lots of goldfish with
lots of orange, black, and white spots.

But none of the fish looked just like
Speckles.
None of the fish followed Martin's finger
when he ran it across the tank.
Martin missed Speckles even more.
"Let's get a fighter fish instead,"
said Brenda.
"These guppies are cute," said Bunny.
"I think we should buy one of these
tiny frogs," said Sammy.
"YOU'RE NOT HELPING!" said Martin.
Just then, RAT came into the store
with Animal on a leash.
"I saw you guys come in here.
What's up?" he asked.

All of a sudden, Animal barked.
He jumped at a parrot and
knocked over a snake tank.
The snake slid toward the white mice
and was going to eat them.

BARK

The pet store man saved
the mice just in time.
"All of you, get out of here now!"
the man shouted.

The boys and girls felt very sad
as they walked back to their homes.
Martin was saddest of all.

Lisa was waiting for Martin at the door.
"Go potty," she said.
"Ask Mommy to take you," said Martin.
"GO POTTY!" Lisa said again.
She led Martin to the bathroom.

There was Speckles!
He was swimming in Lisa's little potty!
Martin gave his sister a big hug.
He carefully carried Speckles back
to the fish tank.

For the rest of the holiday, Martin took
very good care of Ms. Darcy's fish.
When school started, he returned them.
Ms. Darcy was proud of him.
The fish were healthy and safe.

That night, Martin's mother and father
had a surprise for him —
a goldfish of his very own.
Martin named him Speckles Two.